STAT

MOST VALUABLE

STAT

MOST VALUABLE

by AMAR'E STOUDEMIRE

illustrated by TIM JESSELL

SCHOLASTIC INC.

This book is dedicated to all the children around the world who dedicate themselves to excellence.

Stay smart. Believe in school.

*   *   *

Special thanks to Michael Northrop

ISBN 978-0-545-60613-4

Cover and interior art by Tim Jessell
Original cover design by Yaffa Jaskoll

12 11 10 9   17 18 19/0

Printed in the U.S.A.   40

First printing, January 2014

*T*he phone was still ringing out in the hall. I looked across the couch at Junior, like: *You gonna get that?*

My older brother flicked his chin toward the basketball game we were watching. *Are you kidding?*

I nodded. Sometimes brothers don't need to say anything to say a lot.

Finally, the phone stopped ringing and I heard Dad talking in the hall. A minute later, he ducked his head into the room. "Hey, STAT," he said. "It's Overtime."

"What are you talking about?" I said, pointing toward the TV. "It's still the fourth quarter." That's when I figured it out. "Oh, you mean *Overtime* Overtime!"

Dad chuckled and held out the phone. I shot up off

the couch and into the hallway. You didn't keep a street-ball legend like Omar "Overtime" Tanner waiting.

"Hello?" I said when I picked up the phone.

"What's up, STAT?" said Overtime. I thought it was cool that he was using the nickname Dad had given me. It stood for Standing Tall and Talented. Overtime got right down to business after that. "What are you doing the next few weekends?"

I thought about it for a second. I'd probably help out Dad with his lawn-care company, hang out with my friends, and hit the books. "Usual stuff," I said.

"Think you can make time for some hoops?" he said.

"I can always make time for that! You having another tournament?"

"Yeah, the biggest one of the year," he said. "It's the Classic, the fund-raiser that makes all the others possible."

"Oh, man, I've heard of that! Wait, you want me to play in the Classic?"

"You bet I do," he said. "Getting the right mix of play-ers is a big part of what makes it work, and I want to lock up some of you core guys early."

He said some other stuff after that, but I missed it. I was thinking, *I'm a "core guy"?* But after a few moments, I realized there was silence on the other end of the line. He was waiting for an answer.

"I'm in!" I said. As if there was any doubt.

"That's great, Amar'e," he said. "I'll get you the practice schedule and all that once it's set."

After the call, I wandered back into the living room. Dad had taken my spot on the couch and was watching the game. It really was in overtime now. I walked over and stood behind Dad and Junior, checking out the score.

"Don't worry about work," said Dad without peeling his eyes from the action. "You can make it up after the Classic."

"You're playing in the Classic?" said Junior, not turning around, either. "I did that. Cool."

None of us said another word until a half-court shot went wide and the game was officially over. I was thinking how awesome it would be to be in a tourney my brother had played in. It was like a family tradition or something. When the phone rang again, I shot out into the hall and grabbed it on the second ring.

"Hey, man," I heard on the line. I recognized the voice instantly. It was my friend Jammer. His real name was James, but no one had called him that since his first monster dunk. As soon as I heard his voice, I knew why he was calling. He was a "core guy," too!

We talked for a while. We were both wondering who else Overtime would be inviting.

"You going to the old-timers game?" Jammer said after a few minutes. "Overtime and some of the other big names from back in the day are playing a charity game down in Polk City."

"Oh, I gotta see that. When is it?"

"Tuesday at seven."

I did some quick math in my head. That was enough time for me to get back from basketball practice with my school's team and get down there.

"Pretty sure I can get a ride," I said.

"Don't sweat it," said Jammer. "My cousin's driving me. We'll swing by."

And just like that, I had plans for Tuesday — and for the next few weekends.

CHAPTER 2

Before we even reached our seats at Overtime's game, we knew this wasn't going to be any ordinary game. "Young blood!" a booming, amplified voice called out as we scanned the bleachers for open seats.

The voice was coming from a set of outdoor loudspeakers, but we turned to see who was doing the talking. He wasn't hard to find. A man wearing a bright red sports jacket and crazy plaid pants was standing at center court. He was holding a microphone and entertaining the crowd.

"Look at these three young bucks," he said. Jammer was a year older than me, and his cousin Carl was at least sixteen. "Moment they walked in, they lowered the average age by 'bout half!"

There was laughter from the stands, and I couldn't help but smile. This was an old-timers game, and from what I saw, that went for the crowd, too.

"I remember when I was their age," the MC continued. "'Course those memories are a little hazy."

We climbed the rows and found some spots. We scooted past a couple of old-timers. "Excuse me, sir," said Jammer. "Pardon me." He was that kind of guy.

Pretty soon the game got started, and the MC really hit his stride. "Introducing the first team," he bellowed into the mic. "Straight out of Polk County, and possibly fresh out of the ground, it's . . . the Senior Centers!"

The crowd roared with laughter. I scanned the crew taking the court. We saw a lot of gray in their hair but we didn't see Overtime.

"He must be on the other team," said Jammer.

"And introducing their opponents, fighting out of the gray corner, they're . . . Old as Dirt!"

Sure enough, Overtime was in the lead. A lot of the crowd recognized him and cheered a little louder.

"Look at their outfits," said Carl. "Straight out of the seventies!"

Both teams had their socks pulled up to their knees and their shorts pulled halfway up their stomachs. And some of those bellies were as round as the ball. But as soon as the game started, they showed that they'd learned something in all those years.

There were precise cuts, pinpoint passes, and lots of fancy dribbling. It was a good show, and the MC described everything in hilarious detail. A few plays in, Overtime zoomed down the lane. The guy with the ball was facing the other way, but somehow he hit him in stride with a between-the-legs bounce pass.

Overtime's dunking days were over, but he finished with a sweet finger roll. It's true that the defense wasn't exactly knocking itself out on either side, but it was still an impressive bucket. The MC just about lost it.

"Is this a basketball game or a magic show, folks?" he shouted. "Old as Dirt takes the lead! Overtime Tanner with another two points! What's that, OT, one million, lifetime?"

Overtime flashed the MC a big smile and gave him a finger point. It was a nice gesture, but bad timing. One of the Senior Centers was cutting in front of him, following the guy he was supposed to be pretending to guard. OT didn't see him and they bumped knees.

That's always painful, but when you're pushing sixty? The crowd got quiet and Overtime crumbled to the ground. There was a loud *BWONK* as the MC dropped the mic.

Everyone was watching, waiting to see if OT was okay. It didn't look good. He was on the ground, grabbing his knee, and his face was twisted in pain. But he was a gamer. We all knew that. As we watched, his face turned from pain to determination. He called two teammates over. His familiar deep voice carried through the warm Florida air. His teammates bent down and helped him get to his feet. But we all noticed he only used one leg.

With his arms around their shoulders, he hopped over to the sideline. I could tell he didn't want to hold things up or put too much of a damper on the fun. Another old-timer made a big show of taking off his warm-ups.

The MC picked up the mic. He waited for Overtime to give him a thumbs-up and then went back to work. "Well, folks, that's a warrior right there. Let's have a hand for Overtime!"

We all clapped and cheered.

"But the game must go on," the MC continued. "As you know, when the equipment is this old, you need to have a lot of spare parts."

There were gentle chuckles as he introduced OT's replacement. The game went on, maybe just a little more carefully. Jammer and I had seen enough, though. We worked our way down through the bleachers to check on our friend, and Carl tagged along.

It took us a while to get through the crowd. When we finally reached the bench along the sideline, Overtime was nowhere in sight. "'Scuse me," I said to a guy riding the bench, "where's OT?"

"On his way to the hospital," the man said. "Just slipped out so he wouldn't worry anyone."

"Oh, man," I said. "Not good."

Jammer turned to his cousin. "You know how to get to the nearest hospital?"

"I play football for Polk City South," he said. "Of course I do."

CHAPTER 3

Carl drove us over to the hospital. It was the same one I went to when I had hurt my eye during practice. I knew just where to go. "Let's try the emergency room entrance," I said.

We walked through the sliding door and followed the signs for the ER waiting room. There were a dozen people there, but Overtime wasn't one of them.

We tried the main desk next. Carl was in the lead, because he was the oldest. He patted down his hair as we approached the nurse at the desk. "Excuse me, ma'am," he said, sounding a lot like his cousin. "We're looking for someone."

The nurse looked up. "And who might that be, son?" she said.

"Overtime Tanner," said Carl.

The nurse raised one eyebrow. "Overtime?"

"It's Omar, ma'am," I said. She didn't look like much of a hoops fan.

"Omar Tanner," she said, looking down and typing. "Ah, yes, just admitted."

"Great!" said Carl. "Well, not great that he was admitted, but great that . . . Oh, you know."

She gave Carl a concerned look, like she was thinking of admitting him.

Jammer leaned around his cousin. "Uh, what room is he in, ma'am?"

"Room 327-B," she said. "Two flights up."

We hopped into the elevator and took it up to the third floor. The clean, quiet hallway reminded us where we were — and why we were here.

The only sounds were our sneakers on the tile as we worked our way down the room numbers. We turned the first corner and there it was: 327-B. The door was open just a sliver. We could see that the light was on, but that was it.

"Should we knock?" I whispered. "What if he's asleep?"

"What if there's a doctor in there with him?" asked Carl.

We stood there motionless.

"Well, we're here now," whispered Carl. He raised his hand to the door. Before he could knock, we heard a big, deep voice from inside.

"Come on in, boys." It was Overtime.

Carl pushed the door open and we all filed in.

"You've got some good ears," said Carl.

"For an old guy, you mean?" OT managed a smile, to let us know he was just joking. He was lying on a narrow hospital bed, the kind with metal rails on either side. He was wearing a hospital robe and resting on top of the covers.

Jammer, Carl, and I were all athletes, so we all knew the deal: RICE. That stood for Rest, Ice, Compression, and Elevation, and right now, OT was a textbook example. His left knee was bundled up in an enormous ice pack. This thing was the real deal, with a layer of tape and gauze under it, so it wouldn't be right on his skin, and about five more layers over and around it. It looked like his knee was in a big white cocoon.

The bed, ice, and tape took care of the R, I, and C. And the E wasn't just some pillows tossed underneath. His whole leg was hoisted into the air by some cotton straps and a pulley set up over the bed.

"Some setup, isn't it?" he said. That sort of broke the spell and I realized we'd all been staring at it.

"Yeah," I said. "How, uh, how are you feeling?"

"I've felt better," he cracked. He managed another smile, but I could see the effort it took this time. "They're just waiting for the swelling to go down, and then they'll operate."

"Oh, man," said Jammer. "I'm really sorry."

"Me too," said Carl.

I was about to put in my "Me three," but OT held up his hand. "That's all right, boys. I've been through it before. I'm just sorry about the tournament."

Jammer and I looked at each other, then back at OT. "What d'you mean?" we said at exactly the same time.

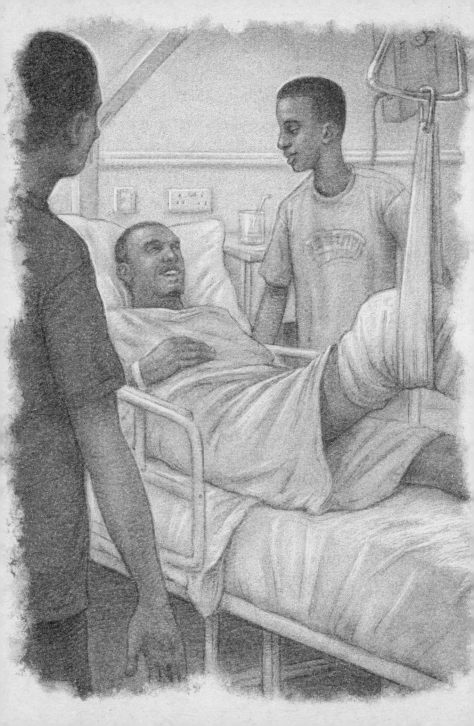

"I'm sorry, boys, but there's no way I can pull the Classic together now. There's just a couple of weeks to go and so much left to do. And, well, I'm in no shape to do it."

I looked down at Overtime's leg. He still moved so well on the court that it was easy to forget how old he actually was. He must've been following my eyes.

"Oh, this old leg is only the half of it," he said. "The doctor wasn't too happy with me when he saw me again. Says I've been 'overdoing' it."

He paused for a moment and then let out a little laugh. "Hard to argue with that!"

I remembered him running full out down the lane and leaping up to lay the ball in.

"I'm on strict orders to take it easy, and I'm afraid the doc might be right about that, too," he said. "You reach my age, you start to get a feel for when you need to listen."

"Oh, man," said Jammer, shaking his head.

"But the Classic's been going on forever," said Carl.

"My older brother even played in it," I said.

"Been going on longer than that," said OT. "Nineteen years and never missed a beat. At first, I thought maybe

I could make the calls from here, but there's more to it. We'd need at least eight teams — good ones — plus practices and promotion and everything else. Nope, nineteen years. Shame we couldn't make it to twenty, but it was a good run."

We were quiet for a while. Jammer and I were both bummed about not getting to play in the Classic together. But more than that, we could tell how much the tourney meant to OT, and what a big loss this was.

Then I started to get a strange feeling. It started down in my chest and rose up like a balloon. It was the feeling I got when I was about to make a big — and possibly crazy — decision. Sure enough, that balloon popped right out of my mouth. "What if you had some help?"

Overtime looked at me. "What's that now?"

"What if you had someone to do all the legwork for you, to make the calls, and to run the practices," I said.

"Yeah," said Jammer. "Someone — or some*ones*."

I looked at my friend and nodded.

"I don't know," said Overtime. "It's an awful lot of work. . . ."

But the more I thought about it, the more I knew. I wouldn't even have met Jammer if it wasn't for OT. For two decades, he'd been making a difference, putting on tourneys, and giving kids around here something positive to work toward. And now, on the twentieth anniversary, that was all supposed to end in some little hospital bed with railings? Not going down like that!

"I don't mind the work," I said.

"I don't, either," said Jammer.

"And I don't mind driving 'em to it!" said Carl. Jammer reached over and bumped fists with his cousin.

A smile spread slowly across Overtime's face. And this time, just for that moment, there wasn't even any pain in it. "Well, if you think you can . . ."

There was a knock at the door. It was the nurse. "Visiting hours are over," she said.

Overtime needed to get his rest, and we needed to let him. I had just one thing left that I needed to say.

"The Classic will happen this year. That's a promise."

A crazy promise, maybe, but a promise just the same.

CHAPTER 4

B R R R R R R R R R R R R R R A N N N N K K K!
BRRRRRRRRANNNNKKK!

The noise filled the classroom. It was so loud, it shook my eardrums. It was third period on Wednesday, and I'd spent most of the day a million miles away, thinking about everything I'd have to do to make the Classic happen. This definitely snapped me out of it.

My best friend Deuce was sitting one desk up. He turned around: "Fire drill."

"Everybody up," called Ms. Lake from the front of the class. "Line up. Single file now."

I got to my feet. Mike, my other best friend, said, "Awesome! I didn't do the homework!"

Deuce and I waved him off. We'd both done ours. And just like that, we were marching out the door.

The hallway was a sea of kids. Our line started moving toward the big double doors that led to the back parking lot.

"Think this is a real fire?" asked Deuce.

"No way," said Mike. "No smoke."

"Yeah, this is a total fire drill," Deuce said.

He was right, too. Ms. Lake had been way too calm when the alarm went off. She must've known it was coming. I was about to say so, but something bigger occurred to me. This was exactly what my life felt like right now: a fire drill. I was just going along, everything normal. Then all of a sudden, I'm scrambling to put together a tournament.

Before I knew it, I was a million miles away again. I started to think about basketball practice today, how maybe I could ask the best guys from the school team to play in the Classic.

"What do you think, Amar'e?" said Deuce.

"Huh?" I said. I looked around and realized we were out in the parking lot already. "Think about what?"

"Man, you are lost in space today," said Deuce.

"Seriously, man," said Mike. "Earth to STAT. Do you read us?"

I shook my head. "Sorry, guys. I just got — well, I agreed to do something last night, something big."

"What is it, man?" said Mike.

They were both leaning in, ready for whatever I was about to say. "It's a lot of work," I said. "I really didn't want to drag you guys into it."

"Come on, man," said Deuce. "We're your best friends."

"Yeah," said Mike. "Consider us dragged."

I looked around. There were hundreds of kids standing out in the bright Florida sunshine, with teachers rushing up and down, trying to keep all the little groups together. Inside, the alarm was still honking. Now that I thought about it, I could use a little help keeping things together, too.

"I'm organizing a big tournament: the Classic," I said.

"I've heard of that," said Mike.

"No sweat," said Deuce.

"Yeah," said Mike. "We'll help you out."

"You don't have to," I said.

"But we're going to," he said.

I looked over at Deuce. He nodded.

All day long, I'd been thinking about the short time and all the things that could go wrong. Now I thought about all the things I had going for me: Jammer working on things on his end, Carl to drive us around, two good friends here, and a tournament everyone had already heard of.

Inside the school, the fire alarm switched off.

"Told you it was a drill," said Deuce, giving Mike a push.

Mike pushed him back, and Deuce spun his arms backward like he was about to fall over.

"Great," I said as our class started shuffling slowly toward the open doors and the cool, dark hallway inside. "Biggest tourney of my life, and I've got a couple of jokers to help me."

"Yeah, you're pretty lucky," Mike said. "Now that you've got us helping, why don't you go find some players for this thing."

CHAPTER 5

*T*WEEEEEEEEEET!

Coach B blew his whistle long and loud. "All right, I've seen enough!" he shouted.

Practice had just started, and he wasn't happy with how it was going. Our school team, the Bears, was pretty good. We were in first place in the league, but just barely.

"We're only one game up on Central," said Coach. "One tiny game! If we want to stay that way, we can't have sloppy passes and lazy cuts. I've been seeing way too many of those lately."

We'd stopped in the middle of a full-court scrimmage, and now we were just standing there. The ball was still rolling around in the corner of the gym, where it had ended up after the last sloppy pass. I risked a quick look over at Isaac. He was our starting point guard and a good one, but, yeah, that was a bad pass. He was staring really hard at his shoelaces, like he was trying to memorize them.

I hadn't done anything too bad today. I mean, I'd missed a shot or two, but I hadn't made any boneheaded plays. I was the only sixth grader on a team of seventh and eighth graders, and I knew from day one I had to avoid those.

"Maybe it was that fire drill," Coach said. "Your bodies came back in the building, but I think your minds might still be out there in the sunshine. Maybe we should have a fire drill of our own."

We all looked around at one another. Even Isaac looked up. None of us had heard of a basketball fire drill before. And whatever it was, we all knew it was going to be intense.

One more long, loud whistle, and we found out just how intense. The rules were pretty simple. It was three-on-three, half-court. The offense inbounded the ball from the sideline and then tried to score, but here's the thing. The offense wasn't allowed to dribble, just pass, and the defense had to play man-to-man, so they couldn't double the person with the ball. With no dribbling, it would take tons of cutting and screening and everything else to get open.

When Coach B told us the rules, some guys laughed and others just shook their heads. But he wasn't done. "Offense has ten seconds to score," he said. He picked up the digital stopwatch that always hung next to his whistle. "Otherwise they stay out there. If they score, the defense stays out. And let me tell you, you'll get awful tired trying to match those fresh legs!"

Now the laughs turned to groans. For some reason, that seemed to make Coach happy. One more whistle — TWEEEEEEEEEET! — and we got to it.

Isaac, Kurt, and Joe, the three involved on that last sloppy play, were on offense first. We all knew that wasn't a coincidence. As I watched them line up, I had something else in mind other than my own group being up next. That last play aside, all three of those guys were good players. And I had a tournament to scout for. I needed eight three-man teams, and they had to be tournament-ready. To get that many, I knew I'd need some Bears in the mix.

Kurt inbounded the ball to Isaac, who used his speed to get open. Then Kurt and Joe both bolted toward the free throw line from opposite directions. Isaac fired the ball to Joe.

Kurt spun around to create some space, and Joe fired the ball to him. The court was strangely silent without dribbling. The only sounds were the squeak of sneakers and the quick breaths of the players.

Kurt had the ball and half a step at the high post. Almost everyone expected him to go up with it, but not me. I'd seen Isaac, still using that speed. He hadn't stopped moving the whole time. Now he burst into the open, cutting toward the hoop from the opposite side.

Kurt hit him in stride with a laser pass. Isaac went up, the ball went in, and the whistle went off.

"That's more like it!" called Coach B.

It was definitely impressive, but I couldn't quite shake the memory of that ball rolling around in the corner. They might be good enough for the Classic. But were they consistent enough?

Isaac, Kurt, and Joe high-fived as they headed toward the sideline. The defenders just shook their heads and waited for the next three. They still had work to do.

So did I. I was one of the next three.

I was ready for this "fire drill" to be over as soon as it began. Two seconds in, I was pinned near the baseline by a bad pass. Now, being pinned near the sideline is bad when you can dribble. When you can't, it's pretty much a dead end. Even worse, Gerry was defending me. He was my closest friend on the team and that meant he knew all my tricks. He was all over me, slapping and grabbing at the ball.

My teammate Anton came back to me, hoping I could get him the ball. Unfortunately, his defender came with him. That was too many hands in too little space. I had to get rid of the ball now or I'd lose it for sure.

My other teammate was Mark Bibo. The good news is he was the best player on the team. The bad news is I couldn't see where he was through all the shifting bodies and flailing arms.

Gerry got one hand on the ball. In another second, he'd get the other one on it, too. I did the only thing I could think of. "Up top!" I shouted as loud as I could. All I could do was hope Bibo heard me.

Then I jumped backward toward the sideline and away from all the grabbing hands. I turned sideways in the air and launched the ball with a hook-shot motion an eye blink before I went out of bounds.

The ball flew in a high, lazy arc toward the air in front of the rim. Suddenly, two hands rose to meet it. Bibo. He'd heard me after all. As the ball dropped past the rim, he stretched out and got the tips of his long fingers on it. It was just enough to tap the ball up and in.

The whistle blew. The defense couldn't believe it. They'd done everything right this time, but they still couldn't get off the court.

"Good D," I said to Gerry. I held out my hand to give him a low five.

"You and Bibo, man," he said, slapping my palm, "you're too tall."

My two teammates caught up with me as we headed up the sideline.

"Thanks for bailing me out," I said to Bibo.

He didn't talk much, but he gave me a quick nod, like: *No problem*.

"Yeah, that was a great play," said Anton.

That wasn't just a great play, I thought as we joined the other players. *That was a Classic play*.

The drill had started off with two quick buckets, but the defense ruled after that. Gerry had had enough. He gambled on the next inbounds pass, rose straight up, and plucked the ball out of the air.

TWEEEEEET!

The group on defense after that was led by Kelvin. He was our starting center and a real space eater. As soon as his guy got the ball down low, he used his powerful hands — seriously, he had Man Hands — to rip the ball loose.

TWEEEEEET!

I took a mental photo of that play. I knew the Classic had to be about more than just high-flying offense. Also, I was the youngest player, but here I was scouting the veterans. They might not like that. Could this work? I needed a plan, fast.

CHAPTER 6

When I got home after practice, I went straight to my room. I rummaged around and found an old notebook that still had some blank pages. Then I started listing names. I gave each one a few lines so I could make notes and things like that.

When I was done, I looked at the list. Even with a few lines for each name, it still looked short. Out in the hall, I heard the screen door creak open and bang shut. Dad was home.

I left the notebook open on my desk and headed out to wash up and get ready for dinner. I gave the little list one last look before ducking out of the room. *At least it's a start*, I told myself.

We had garlic smashed potatoes with dinner. I loved those — and Junior loved pretty much anything. We were having a pretty good fencing match with our spoons for the last scoop when the phone started ringing. Neither of us so much as looked in that direction — that's how duels are lost.

Dad let out a long sigh, and got up and got it. "It's for you, STAT," he called from the hall.

As I got to my feet, Junior scooped up the last lump of smashed potatoes and began savoring his victory.

"Thanks, Dad," I said, taking the phone.

"It's Jammer."

"Oh, cool," I said. Junior could have his potatoes. I had business to discuss.

"'Sup, player?" said Jammer.

We joked around for a few minutes and then got down to business.

"Got us a practice court," said Jammer. "You know the one just off Palmer? Remember we played that one tourney there?"

"Yeah, that's a nice one," I said. It was part of a fancy

sports complex and you had to make reservations for it and all that. "How'd you snag it?"

"I almost didn't. It was like the third place I tried, and they weren't really having it. But then I mentioned it was for Overtime, and it was like magic. They scheduled us for the next two Saturdays."

"What about the one after that, the actual tournament?"

"Nah, I wish. They're booked that whole weekend."

"I guess we've still got time for that," I said. "At least we have someplace good to practice."

"Yeah," said Jammer. "Now all we need is some players to do the practicing."

"Seriously," I said. I pictured my short list. "You got anyone?"

"A few," he said. "I tracked down the other 'core guys' OT already invited."

"Nice," I said. "Who are they?"

"Round Mound!" he said.

"Should've known!" I said. "Of course he'd want Khalid out there."

Khalid was a friend of ours — and a great point guard. He didn't look it. He was a little plump around the edges, which is how he got his nickname, but all that did was give him the permanent element of surprise. He was actually super-quick, with a first step you wouldn't believe. "Who else?" I said.

"Stevie, too," said Jammer.

"Makes sense," I said. He was tall and versatile, the kind of guy who could play every position on the court. "And?"

"Braylon and Benoit."

Braylon I knew. He was a deadly outside shooter, but I'd never heard of the other one. "Who's Benoit?"

"No idea. Khalid says he's new around here."

"From where — France?"

"Yeah, right? Michigan, I think, or somewhere like that. Supposed to be the real deal, though."

"Okay, cool. Who else?"

"That's it."

"That's it?"

"Yeah, what do we have, a bad connection?"

"No, I heard you," I said. "It's just . . ."

"Yeah, it's not a lot," said Jammer. "Four guys, plus us. That's just two teams. Still have six to go."

"Man," I said. "And that's only if they all show up."

"Man," he agreed. "How many have you come up with?"

So I told him about the names in my notebook: three guys, maybe four at the most. "Plus me," I added.

"We already counted you," said Jammer. "You can only play for one team."

"Oh yeah," I said. "So that's one more team, with maybe a guy left over."

"If they all agree and aren't busy."

We were both quiet for a while, thinking the same thing: three teams down — maybe — at least five to go.

"I guess I could lower the bar a little," I said.

"No way," said Jammer. "Remember, these guys don't have to meet our standards; they have to meet Overtime's."

He was right. I thought about what Overtime would've thought if he'd watched Bears practice today. I felt pretty confident he would've written down the same names I had.

"All right," said Jammer. "So we still got some work to do. We got a little time, and I think there are a few guys at my school I could ask. You've asked your guys, right?"

Before I could admit I hadn't, a big shadow fell over me in the hall. I looked up and saw Dad. "Doing all this talking," he said. "That homework better be done."

He looked straight at me, waiting for my answer. I slowly shook my head side to side: nope. Dad was a pretty reasonable guy, and a lot of the rules around the house were pretty flexible. Homework wasn't one of them.

"Jammer," I said, "I gotta go."

I hung up and headed straight to my room. I had English and history homework to do. Those were two of my favorite subjects, but all I could think about was math. Three times five, minus one . . . Where were we going to find that many Classic-type players? I hadn't asked any of my picks yet. What if they said no? The first practice was just a few days away.

CHAPTER 7

*T*hat crazy drill at practice on Wednesday was a good start, but I needed more evidence before I made my final decisions. I remembered what Jammer had said: These guys had to meet OT's standards, not ours. I was also hoping that another player or two would prove themselves, and I could add them to my too-short list.

I felt like a secret agent as I changed for practice on Thursday. My practice jersey was my disguise. My sneakers were my wheels. My goggles were my surveillance gear. My teammates had no idea that I was undercover.

Coach did his part, too. As soon as we were done

warming up, he called out, "Scrimmage! Let's run some full court!"

That was perfect. Drills were fine for scouting, but games were better. We divided up into odds and evens, based on our jersey numbers. I was Team Odd — Number 1. We had one cocaptain, Bibo, and the even team had the other, Kurt. The rest of the talent was divided up pretty evenly.

Bibo jumped halfway to the roof to win the opening tip and we were off and running. I zoomed down the court, trying to space the floor and get open. Gerry was running the point for us, and he pulled up near the free throw line. I kept going and tried to carve out some position down low.

Kelvin was already there, clogging the lane with his big frame. I got in front of him and Gerry fired the ball to me. As soon as I got it, I felt Kelvin's forearm in my back. It was like a steel beam. The message: You're not getting any closer. I could go for a hook shot or maybe try to get him to bite on an up and under, but the scout in me had other ideas.

I saw Bibo flashing into the high post and fired the

ball back out to him. Joe was defending him and had good position, but it didn't matter. Bibo went from going full-speed forward to full-speed sideways in the space of one jump stop.

Joe was left standing there, his feet planted like petunias and his arms pressed to his sides, waiting for a charge that never came. Bibo slid by and scored easily.

One bucket in, and Bibo was already a lock for an invitation. In my mind, I put a little check by his name on my list. As I headed back up the court on defense, I reached back and rubbed my lower back. Kelvin had made a strong "first impression" himself.

Kurt had the ball for the other team, and I watched him closely. He was another candidate, but he fired up a brick. I didn't hold it against him: We all missed, especially from that far out. But as the game went on, I started to notice something else. It wasn't just that he was missing more shots than he was making. He was a streaky shooter, and I'd seen games where he hit everything. It was that he was getting really down on himself when he missed. His jaw clenched up and his shoulders slumped.

When he fired up another shot that barely drew iron, I knew he was beating himself. No check mark there. But all the open looks Kurt was getting were coming from somewhere: Isaac. He was running the other team's offense smoothly and getting good looks for their top guy on the outside.

The next trip up, he looked inside instead. He'd seen the same body language I had and knew he had to adjust his strategy. He hit Kelvin down low with a beautiful bounce pass, and the big man split a double-team to power it up and in.

I'd seen everything I needed to see. Isaac had the smarts to go with his speed, and Kelvin had the O to go with his D. Check and check.

That was three guys. I looked around the court, hoping for at least one more. Gerry was a good point guard, but Isaac was a little better. I was thinking how great it would be to grab a really good forward, when I nearly ran into one.

Joe set a quick screen that I just barely got around. He was sneaky like that. I suddenly realized what a great job he was doing. He had the toughest job on the court, guarding Bibo. No one could shut him down completely, but he'd done a solid job of making him work for every shot and limiting the damage. Meanwhile, he'd been scoring here and there himself, taking advantage of his long arms and good range on his jumper.

I'd made up my mind about Bibo so early that I'd almost missed the rock-solid guy guarding him. Joe was the fourth guy. My secret-agent work was over. I crashed the glass hard and hauled in a rebound. The next trip up on offense, I slipped into the lane and scored.

We ended practice with wind sprints. It seemed kind of cruel — we'd been sprinting all day! But it was still easier than what I had to do next. I was the only sixth grader on the team, and now I had to convince four of the best seventh and eighth graders to play with me in a tournament.

Would they believe me? Would they agree? Would the other players be mad? Was it really a good idea to pass over one of the team captains? There were plenty of questions but not plenty of time. The locker room always cleared out fast.

I took a deep breath and headed in.

CHAPTER 8

"**H**ey, Isaac!" I shouted, and that right there was the problem.

It was chaos in the locker room, with everyone changing clothes and swapping stories, and everything else. I had to shout to be heard, and I didn't really want to shout this.

Isaac was in front of his locker, talking to his friend Deek. I knew Deek pretty well, too. Sometimes we studied together down at the library. And he was a good player, just not quite good enough for the Classic. That was no insult. Nine out of ten good players weren't up to OT's standards. But it wasn't necessarily something you wanted to shout in his face, either.

"What's up, Amar'e?" said Isaac.

"Yeah, what's up, man?" said Deek.

I looked at both of them. "Uh, nothing," was all I could think to say.

They gave me a weird look. If I could, I probably would've given myself a weird look, too. But right then I spotted Bibo on his own. He was a better bet. He was a quiet guy who let his game do the talking. Sometimes he'd go entire practices without saying a word. He was definitely less likely to be talking to someone in the locker room.

I headed straight for him, but I got cut off halfway. "Hey, Amar'e," I heard. I turned and there was Gerry, holding up a nickel. "Look what I found."

I didn't want to miss Bibo, but I didn't want to be rude, either. When I first joined the team, Gerry was the first guy to talk to me. He was a good friend. "A nickel?" I said.

"Yeah, but check it out," he said. He pushed the thing closer to my face, but it still looked like a nickel to me. "It's from 1935!"

"Whoa!" I said. I'd never seen one that old before. That was before World War II. And now that I looked closer, it did seem different.

"Think it's worth anything?"

"Maybe," I said. "I'll give you a dime for it."

"You wish," he said.

I was about to up my offer to a quarter, but I shot a quick look over at Bibo's locker. It was closed and he was gone.

"Aw, man!" I said.

"Yeah, that's right," said Gerry. "This thing'll cost you a sack of dimes!"

I gave him an out-of-my-price-range smile and left him standing there, holding his new treasure up to the light. I caught sight of Bibo by the door, and made a quick turn. For the second time that day, I nearly ran into Joe.

"Joe!" I said.

"That's my name," he said.

The locker room was starting to clear out around us, and the volume had dropped enough that I could talk at a more normal level. "Ever think about playing in a tournament?" I started.

"Thought about it," he said, "but I've always just played on the team."

"You could do both," I said. "At least this one time."

"What one time?"

So I told him. I just rattled it off in the center of the room, as players passed by on either side.

"The Classic, huh?" he said.

"Yeah, it's —" I started, but he cut me off.

"I know what it is," he said. "It's Overtime Tanner's thing."

"Yeah!" I said. "I'm kind of helping him out."

"Cool," said Joe. "I'm in."

"Great!" I said, and then gave the locker room another quick look. Bibo was gone and Isaac's locker was closed now. Kelvin was putting his backpack on near the door.

"Who else?" said Joe. He must've read my mind, or at least my eyes.

"Bibo, Isaac, and Kelvin," I said.

He thought about it for a second and nodded. "Yeah, that's who I'd pick, too."

I was happy to hear that, and even happier to hear what he said next. "Yo, Bibo!" he shouted. "Isaac! K-man!"

His words echoed through the locker room.

Isaac appeared from somewhere behind us. "What's up, Joe?" he said.

Kelvin stopped in his tracks by the door: "Yeah?"

Those three were all eighth graders and knew one another pretty well.

A second later, Bibo ducked his head back into the locker room. Being Bibo, he didn't say anything. Instead, he looked at us and raised one eyebrow higher than the other, the universal expression for *What's up?*

I gave all three of them a big, wide smile, the universal expression for *I think you're going to like this.*

I thought I might have to convince some of them, but they'd all heard of the Classic, or at least had heard of Overtime. OT might have been chilling at the hospital, I thought as I gave them all the details about the first practice, but his name was sure opening a lot of doors.

On Friday, Deuce used his nerd connections to score Mike and me passes to the computer lab during class.

"Special project," he said to our teacher. She really liked Deuce, so she let us have some extra time in there.

Now that there were some actual players, it was time to think about getting an actual crowd. A fund-raising tournament needed paying customers.

Our school didn't exactly have cutting-edge technology when it came to computers. The one we were using kept freezing up, and even Deuce wasn't sure how to use the graphics program.

The "technical difficulties" burned a lot of time, and we burned more looking for cool images and artwork to include. Then we spent about ten minutes trying to decide what the flyer should say. Deuce thought we should put *The Classic's Back!* in huge type at the top. Mike wanted it to say *The One, the Only, the Classic!*

Those were both good, but I had my own idea. "How about *20 Years of Classic Action*?" I said.

Mike and Deuce looked at each other and nodded. "Yeah," said Mike. "Let's go with that."

We were still trying to figure out how big we could get the type when the warning bell went off.

"We'll finish next time," said Deuce.

"Yeah, there are still some little details to iron out, anyway," I said.

"Like what?" said Deuce.

"Oh, you know, like if we'll have a court or enough players or if it will even happen," I said.

"And if anyone will show up if it does," added Mike.

"Okay," said Deuce. "As long as it's nothing major."

CHAPTER 9

It was 9:45 on Saturday morning, and I was at the practice space at the sports complex. The court had freshly painted lines and not a crack in sight. It was perfect, but it was also empty.

Practice was supposed to start in fifteen minutes, and the only people here were the ones I'd come with. Jammer was standing next to me, dribbling a ball slowly, just warming up. Carl was next to him, his car keys dangling from one finger. Mike and Deuce were walking around checking out the court. I'd asked them to come as a favor. I figured they could fill in if a few people didn't show up. Now it was starting to look like no one would.

"You, uh, want me to stick around?" Carl said to Jammer.

We all knew what he meant: If no one showed, he could just drive us home.

"Nah," said Jammer. "They'll be here. Still got fifteen minutes."

He looked over at me for backup. "Yeah," I said. "The invitations were pretty last-minute. They're probably just arranging rides and stuff."

Carl took one last look around the empty court. "If you say so," he said. He flipped his keys off his finger and up into the air, then caught them in his hand and headed for the parking lot. "Be back at eleven thirty."

I looked over at Jammer. "They'll be here," he said. "I got a couple guys who told me they'd definitely show."

"Don't sweat it," said Mike. He'd made it all the way around the court and back again. "We can just run two-on-two."

We heard Carl pull his car out of the lot. As we turned to look, another car pulled in from the other direction.

"All right!" said Jammer.

It was a tiny two-door Ford, but when it started unloading people, it was like a clown car at a circus. Four people got out, and most of them looked way too tall to have gotten in that little thing in the first place.

It was the three players from Jammer's school, along with one of their moms. The boys stretched out their long limbs, just to make sure everything still worked. Then they headed toward the court with the mom in the lead.

"Think she plays?" I said to Jammer.

He was smiling now. His people had shown up, and we had enough to at least run threes.

The cars started coming one after another then. I recognized Khalid's folks' car as soon as it turned off the highway. A blue car with a pizza-delivery sign on the top pulled up next.

"Someone order a pizza?" said Mike, who was always ready for a meal.

The passenger-side door opened and Kelvin appeared.

"No," I said. "A center."

The car rose a good foot on its springs as soon as he stepped out. He was the first Bear. I felt like I'd just drained a big three. Jammer hadn't seen Kelvin before, and he was impressed. "Nice," he said.

Stevie and Braylon showed up in the same car after that. Some people knew one another already, and others were introducing themselves. There were high fives and handshakes going on all over the court.

"Who're we still waiting for?" said Khalid after he'd made the rounds and said his hellos.

I looked around. "That new guy, Benoit," I said.

"Oh, he's not coming," said Khalid. "I talked to him last night. He can't make it today."

"That's too bad," I said. I was pretty curious to see this new "core guy."

"So is that it?" said Khalid. I could see him looking around the court, counting with his eyes. It was the same way he sized up the defense on the fly during games.

"No," I admitted. "We're still waiting on three Bears."

"Three bears?" said Khalid, his eyes lighting up. "Is Goldilocks going to be here, too?"

The guys around us all laughed, but not me. It bothered me that the last three guys to show were the ones I'd invited. I was glad that at least Kelvin had made it.

"Should we just get started?" said Jammer. "We've got enough to at least —" But before he could finish his sentence, one last vehicle headed down the road toward the court. It was the Bears, but I couldn't believe who was driving.

"Is that your dad?" said Deuce.

It was. As he turned his old truck into the lot, I could see his familiar outline at the wheel. Bibo and Isaac were in the cab next to him, and Joe was bouncing along in the back, with a big smile on his face. It was pretty fun to ride back there, and it was totally safe since Dad never went much faster than thirty-five.

I headed straight out to the parking lot. This was a story I had to get firsthand. Dad just shrugged and hooked a thumb toward Isaac. "He called the house to say they were going to be late, waiting on a ride," he said. "You'd already left, so I told 'em, 'I can give you a lift.'"

Isaac nodded. "Yep," he said. "Pretty much."

"But you're going to be late for work," I said to Dad. Saturdays were always busy for him.

"I can't be too late," he said with a smile. "I'm the boss!"

He went over and talked a little bit with that one player's mom. She was sticking around to keep an eye on things, and I think he was just reassuring her that we were okay. Then he headed off to work and we got down to business.

Picking teams wasn't an issue. We'd basically arrived in teams. The first was made up of the three guys from Jammer's school: Lex, Van, and Hector. The Bears were trickier, because there were four of them. Joe solved that. "I'll play with anyone," he said. "I already carry these guys on the school team. Let's see if they can play without me."

Even Bibo laughed at that one.

Mike pointed at Deuce and said, "Come play with us."

Joe sized them up and nodded. Mike was a big dude. "Sounds good to me."

That left the three other "core guys," another natural team, with Jammer and me to ref, size up the teams, sub in, and do everything else to make sure we got the most out of the time we had left on the court.

With the teams set, Jammer leaned over toward me and said, "What do you think, half-court or full?" I thought about it. With half-court, all four teams could play at once. But the Classic would be full court.

"Definitely full," I said.

The teams were already talking strategy.

Jammer nodded, then yelled, "Full court, winner stays!"

The first game was Bibo and the Bears versus the guys from Jammer's school. Jammer tossed the opening tip up in the air, and the Lions and Bears began battling.

It was a good game. Lex was as fast as Isaac, and Hector was a lock-down defender who did a great job of staying with Bibo. The difference was in the middle: Van just didn't have the size to handle Kelvin.

The Bears stayed out. Khalid and crew headed out to try to knock them off. It was another good game, and I should know because I was the ref. I didn't need a whistle or anything. Every once in a while, I just had to say a few words. "That was too much banging, K-man," or "You got him on the arm, Khalid."

I could tell right away that the Bears were a little tired. It was the first all-day tourney for some of these guys and they'd just learned lesson number one: Pace yourself. The other team was fresher and knew how to recover during the natural rhythms of the game.

More important, Stevie knew how to defend Kelvin. He wasn't big enough to muscle him, either. But he was faster and had longer arms. He did a good job of fronting him and denying him the ball, and pestering him with his quick hands when he did get it.

Isaac and Khalid were more interested in setting things up than scoring. That all led up to one thing: a fireworks display between Bibo and Braylon on the outside. When the smoke cleared, it was the tourney vets who bested the Bears — but not by much.

Mike, Deuce, and Joe took the court. I wouldn't say this to them, but my first thought was: *I hope they can handle it*. Mike and Deuce were just filling in. They weren't on the school team yet. And Joe was the last guy I'd picked from the Bears. Could be rough.

Shows what I know. Right from the opening tip, they came out strong. At first I thought, *Okay, they've got fresh legs.* But as the game went on, they hung tough. I joke with Mike a lot about his appetite and all that, but he was the only other guy here who really had the size and strength to play Kelvin straight up.

And Deuce had always been quick. I watched him hit Joe with a sweet bounce pass and suddenly I realized: Most of my game came from all the time I'd spent playing hoops with those two. We'd just been playing for fun, but we'd been playing hard. And Joe was another guy like Stevie: He could do it all on the court.

In fact, they were only down a few points when Stevie took a tumble in the lane. It looked pretty bad, and I held my breath for a second. We didn't have enough players to start losing them.

Khalid and I helped Stevie to his feet. I was seriously relieved when he was able to hobble over to the bench under his own power. Jammer came in for Stevie, and his team pulled away after that. Jammer was fresh, and Jammer was, well, Jammer. The guy practically had wings.

Cars had started arriving to pick people up. The games had been good, and guys were already talking about what they were going to do next time.

For a few minutes, I felt pretty good about things, but then Jammer brought me back to reality. "These guys look good," he said. "But we're still seriously short of teams. We had four today, and the Classic's always had eight."

"What do you think about Mike and Deuce?" I said, feeling a flash of pride for my friends.

"Yeah," he agreed. "Let's bring 'em on. They showed they can hang with anyone. . . . But we're still only half-way there."

CHAPTER 10

I got up early on Sunday to help Dad out at work. Because I didn't have enough to do, right? I really didn't mind that much, though. He'd helped me out yesterday giving the guys a lift to practice. And I was used to it, anyway. Most kids helped out around the house. I just helped out around other people's houses, specifically out in the yard.

We loaded up the truck and stopped to pick up Manny on the way to the job. He'd been working with Dad forever and a half, and he wore the same kind of goggles for clipping bushes that I wore for playing hoops.

There were a few more guys at the work site, and I knew them, too. I sort of felt like one of the guys when

I worked with Dad's crew. Everyone had their own job and it made the whole operation go faster.

After we got done, we did the whole thing in reverse: loading the truck back up, dropping Manny off, unloading at home. . . . Then I took a much-needed shower. Before my hair was even dry, the phone started ringing.

Junior and I both charged for it and almost collided. I got there a step ahead of him. When the phone rang at this time on Sunday, we both knew who it was. Junior slunk off to the living room and waited his turn.

"Hi, Mom," I said.

"Hey, Amar'e!"

She was living up in New York State with my little brother. These Sunday calls were mostly just to catch up, but she had a sixth sense for when something was bothering me, too. "Everything good in school?" she was saying.

"Yep," I said.

"How are those grades?"

"Good."

"And how about out of school?"

"Okay," I said. "Kind of."

And just like that, I could feel her locking in.

"And why's that?" she said.

"Well, there's this tournament I'm helping with."

"Mmm-hmmm," she said.

And that's all it took for me to tell her the whole thing.

"So you've asked all the people you know and you only have half the people you need?" she said, summing it up a lot better than I had.

"Yeah, that's pretty much it."

"Well, let me ask you something," she said. "Those other tournaments you played in, or going out for the school team, did you know all those players?"

"No way," I said. "I still don't really know a lot of —"

Suddenly, I got what she was saying. So far, I'd asked all the best players I knew, and Jammer had done the same. If we wanted to drum up enough players, we were going to have to open things up a lot more. Immediately, players came to mind. A sweet scorer who'd given the Bears fits when we played Central. A long, lean defender who'd given me a ton of trouble in that same game. Then other players, from other teams.

"Amar'e, baby? You still there?"

"Yeah, yeah," I said. "Thanks, Mom. You're the best."

"You know I'm always here for you."

I always knew that. "Hey, Mom," I said. "Is the little big man there?"

"Sure is," she said, and she went to get my half brother.

I couldn't talk to him for too long, because Junior was hovering around waiting. Once he got on the phone, I was the one waiting. I had to give Jammer a call. I had a question for him: *Who are the toughest guys you've faced this year?*

The next week flew by. After practice on Monday, the other Bears and I put our heads together to decide who else to invite to the Classic. I asked Kelvin who battled him the toughest down low and Isaac who did the best job of slowing him down. I asked Bibo and Joe who defended them the best — and who they had the toughest time defending.

The locker room cleared out around us as we huddled up and talked it over. Sometimes the guys mentioned names I knew, players from teams we'd already faced that season. Sometimes the names were new to me, guys they'd faced last year, players who'd already been tough in seventh grade and would be back again this year.

Either way, if enough heads started nodding when a name was mentioned, I figured they were the real deal. I wrote the names down on a new sheet in the same notebook where I'd written my first list. So much had happened since then and I still had a lot to get done.

Pretty soon, we had a good list. Then we had to figure out how to contact them. "Anyone know Muni's last name?" I asked. "Wait, *is* that his last name? And what about Fabrice?"

Both of them played for our archrivals, the Central Cougars. I looked around and everyone was shaking his head no. "I always just call him Muni," said Joe. "They always call him that, too."

"Wait a sec," said Isaac. "All that stuff's in the paper."

"Oh yeah," I said. "That's right." The local paper always wrote up the Bears games — and they always used full names. Bibo was Mark Bibo; Joe was Joe Hanlon. The piece on our win over the Cougars would solve the mystery of Muni. They had a stack of old issues in the library, and I was pretty sure it was all online, anyway.

I looked down at my list, a mix of first names, last names, and nicknames. Those old stories would have the answers.

"Thanks, guys," I said as we all grabbed our stuff and headed out of the locker room.

"No problem," said Kelvin.

"Yeah," said Joe. "It'll be awesome to take on some Cougars in the Classic!"

For the rest of the week, I got busy making that happen. I switched into detective mode and did some digging. That's what I was doing after practice Tuesday when a familiar car screeched to a stop in the driveway. By the time I got to the door, I saw Jammer heading my way. Carl was waiting in the car, so I knew we were going somewhere.

"Think we got a court for the game," said Jammer. "You should come check it out."

I gave him a suspicious look. "Why, is there something wrong with it?"

"Just come on," he said, waving me toward the car. He had his poker face on and wasn't giving anything away.

"Hold on," I said. "Let me tell my dad — and get my sneakers."

The trip was familiar right from the start. I knew every turn we were going to take before Carl even signaled. And things were just as familiar once we got there. I climbed out of the car. "This is the court where Overtime got hurt," I said.

"Yep," said Jammer. "Pretty nice one, too."

I looked around. I was half seeing it as it was now and half remembering how it had been that night, flooded with light and sound and packed with people. It was definitely a nice court. But . . .

"Isn't it, I don't know, a little weird?" I said. "I mean, it's his tournament, and this probably isn't his favorite place right now."

Carl shook his head. "Man, at OT's age, if he held it against every court he'd gotten banged up on, he couldn't so much as shoot a free throw without leaving the state."

That seemed like a pretty good point, and it wasn't like we could ask him. The last time we'd tried to call him, that same nurse had given us strict orders not to "pester him with basketball stuff."

"Yeah," said Jammer. "OT would just want the best court possible. And this is it. We can even use the sound system from last time."

"Yeah, that was nice," I admitted. We wouldn't have some guy clowning around and making jokes into the mic during games, but it would be perfect for calling out the action, announcing winners and matchups and all that other stuff. "How'd you get it, anyway?"

A sly smile appeared on Jammer's face. "A little guilt goes a long way," he said.

"What, you guilt-tripped 'em?" I said.

"Not exactly," he said. "I pointed out that Overtime was in the hospital and that his big tournament still didn't have a court lined up. I mean, I might have mentioned where he got hurt a few times. Just, you know, in case they'd forgotten."

"You're an operator, man," I said, breaking out into a smile of my own.

"Never said I wasn't."

I took another long look around the court.

"I think we should have it at night," I said. "Under the lights."

"Definitely."

CHAPTER 11

Deuce was acting all cagey in homeroom on Wednesday, so I knew something was up. I waited him out. Finally, he looked both ways like he was undercover and slid a piece of paper across the top of my desk. "What, are we passing notes now?"

"Just look at it."

I looked down again and said, "It's blank."

He looked at me to see if I was messing with him. I was, but I don't think I gave it away. Finally, he reached over and flipped the paper right side up.

"Whoa!" I said. "This is awesome."

That's when I realized Mike was standing on the

other side of my desk. They were both admiring their work, and I was, too. It was a sweet flyer. It said *20 Years of Classic Action* in big type at the top, just like we'd planned. Then there was an awesome action shot and all the info: the address of the new court and the date and time. They'd even included a "suggested contribution," since this was OT's big fund-raiser for his other tourneys.

"You guys work fast," I said. I'd only given them the info the day before. "Thanks!"

"What?" said Mike. "Who says this is for you? Now that we're going to be playing, we want to make sure we have an audience."

"Yeah," said Deuce. "We owe it to our public!"

I waved them off, but I had to admit it. Of all the invitations I'd handed out for the Classic, being able to invite Mike and D was the best.

"Now," I said. "We just need to figure out where to make a whole mess of copies."

"I got that," said Deuce, reaching over and taking the flyer back. "Trust me."

I looked over at Mike and gave him a look, like: *Do*

you know what he's up to? He shook his head. "I think the less we know about this, the better."

For the rest of the day, the tourney took a backseat to the upcoming Bears game. We were playing the Lake South Gators tomorrow, and it was time to buckle down and really focus on that. Everyone kind of knew it, too. The guys playing in the Classic stopped asking me for updates and double-checking details.

The game was at Lake South. In the locker room before tip-off, Coach B reminded us what was at stake.

"The Gators have one loss," he says. "That means they're only one game behind us. If they win: Bam! They're in first place. And you know who's in second?"

"Us?" said Kelvin.

Coach shook his head and waited a moment, just to build the drama. "The Gators' only loss came from the Cougars. That means if we lose, the Cougars are in second and we're in third."

There was some rumbling in the room. We definitely couldn't have that. Dropping from first all the way to third? And having our archrivals leapfrog us?

"No way!" shouted Kelvin, jumping up off the bench.

Then we all stood up. "Not gonna happen!" said Isaac. Even Bibo chimed in with a loud "Uh-uh."

We took the court knowing what was at stake — but so did the Gators. They could smell first place and were even more fired up by their home crowd. They started off turbocharged, running full out and throwing themselves at every loose ball.

"Weather the storm!" shouted Coach. "Weather the storm!"

We all knew what he meant. They call Florida the Sunshine State, but we had more than our share of big storms down here. But even the biggest storms blow over. We knew if we could keep it close for the first five minutes or so, the Gators' energy level would come back down to earth.

To do it, we needed to stay tough on defense and score enough to keep pace. On both ends of the court, we had to battle a bunch of hyped-up Gators on the boards.

Their top defender was legit. His name was Walter, and he was trading off on Bibo and me. He was doing a good job, but I figured all that switching off could get pretty confusing. And I knew just how to make it worse. The next time the ball sailed out of bounds, I walked over to Isaac. "How about a pick-and-roll with Bibo and me?" I whispered.

He got it immediately. "Yeah," he said. "Definitely."

It worked like a charm. I set the screen for Bibo, and with both of us right next to each other, Walter hesitated just enough. The fact that he recognized the possible pick-and-roll just made it worse. He knew who had the ball now, but not who'd end up with it. He stayed on Bibo, and one of the other defenders jumped up out of his area.

I rolled to the hoop with a patch of court all to myself. Plenty of room to catch a quick pass from Bibo and drain a short jump shot.

The next time up, we did the same thing. This time Walter switched onto me — and Bibo kept the ball and scored.

We didn't do anything fancy on the defensive end, just battled and tried to be smart. They were crashing the boards like crazy. We responded by getting position and boxing out.

Add it all up, and we held our own. Sure enough, Coach was right. After five or six minutes of total intensity, the Gators started to go flat. Their energy level started to drop like the air going out of a balloon. Meanwhile, the score was tied, and we felt like we were just hitting our stride.

We took the lead a minute later, and cruised into halftime with an eight-point cushion. Things were going pretty well, but then it happened. It was right after the half. I was getting a quick rest on the bench, so Bibo was battling Walter one-on-one. Kelvin put up a hook shot that rimmed out. Bibo and Walter went up high to grab the rebound. Bibo got his hands on it first, but the two bumped bodies in midair, and Bibo came down wrong.

"Uh-oh," said the guy next to me on the bench. I hissed some air in through my teeth, and Coach just dropped his head. Bibo had turned his ankle — a lot. For a split second, it looked like he was standing on the side of his sneaker instead of the bottom of it. Now he was on the ground, curled up and holding his ankle.

The whistle blew and half a dozen adults rushed onto the court.

The rest of the game was a blur. Now I was the one battling it out with Walter. During time-outs and breaks in the action, little bits of news trickled in: "looks bad," "on his way to the hospital," "X-rays."

We were all worried about Bibo. He wasn't just a great player, he was a really good guy, too. When I first joined the team, I was the new kid and the only sixth grader. Some of the players gave me a really hard time. But not Bibo. He stuck up for me and passed me the ball.

He made a difference for me, and for other players, too. Some of the guys were pretty emotional on the court. During a time-out, Isaac looked at us and said, "This game's for Bibo." From that point on, the Gators had no shot. We finished the game with the kind of energy they'd started it with and won by twelve.

Afterward, we got the official word: a high-ankle sprain. We were glad nothing was broken, but high-ankle sprains were bad news.

"How long will he be out?" asked Isaac after the game.

Coach looked around the locker room. We'd all stopped moving — practically stopped breathing — waiting to hear the news. "Tough to say," he said. "At least three weeks."

Isaac looked down at the floor and then up at me. We both knew the deal. With a little luck, the Bears would get Bibo back for the play-offs. But the Classic had just lost one of its best players.

CHAPTER 12

On the bus ride home, we were all trying to process the same thing: a big win and a big loss in the same game.

As we pulled out onto the highway, I was thinking about that first pick-and-roll Bibo and I had pulled off against the Gators' defense. That reminded me of Walter. The last time I saw him wasn't on the court; it was outside the locker room after the game. He came up to me and said, "Man, I feel terrible about what happened."

"Not your fault," I told him.

"Yeah?" he said, and seemed to relax a little. "I didn't see him land. We bumped pretty good going up for that ball, and I think coming down, too."

"That's just basketball, man," I said. Walter was a fierce defender, but he didn't seem like a dirty one.

"Thanks," he said, "but I still feel bad. Can you tell him sorry for me?"

"Sure," I said. "I can do that."

It would be no problem to spot Bibo in the hallway at school now. I wondered if he'd be on crutches, or maybe in a boot for a while. As I was thinking that, Walter pulled a scrap of paper out of his pocket. There was just one word on it, *Walter*, and his telephone number.

"Just let me know if he's okay, like if it's not as bad as they think, or whatever," he said. "And let me know if there's anything I can do."

I looked down at the phone number. I already knew he'd probably end up taking Bibo's place at the tourney, but I couldn't deal with that right then. "Sure," I said, and he walked away.

Puhlll-DUMMP! PING! The bus cratered out in a pot-hole. The noise brought me back to the here and now. I looked over at Isaac in the seat across from me. He slid over like he had a secret to tell me.

"I was just talking with Kelvin," he said, looking me straight in the eyes. "Bibo's out, so you're playing with us now, right?"

The question caught me by surprise — and it put me in a seriously awkward position. I mean, I was a Bear, riding the team bus. But I had other friends in the tourney, too: Jammer and Khalid, and Mike and Deuce, especially.

"The Bears have got to win this tournament," said Isaac, getting tired of waiting for my answer. I had to say something.

"That would be awesome," I said.

"You mean it?"

"Yeah, I mean . . . It would be awesome if the Bears won the Classic."

I was dodging, and Isaac was trying to pin me down.

"So you'll play with Kelvin and me?"

"And then Joe could keep playing with Mike and Deuce," I said, thinking out loud. It made sense, and it seemed like the teams would work. The thing is, right from the start, I'd sort of assumed I'd be playing with

Jammer. And I'm pretty sure he assumed the same thing.

"So," said Isaac. "Yes or no?"

He wanted a decision, but I hadn't even thought about it. It had only been like an hour or so since Bibo got hurt.

"I don't know," I said. "I think I might still have to referee and all that on Saturday."

Isaac looked at me, trying to figure me out. "I'm not talking about the practice," he said.

I knew that, but it was all I had for him.

"We'll figure it out," I said. "All that other stuff will —"

Isaac didn't look satisfied. "Come on. You have to."

Luckily, we were just about home. I grabbed my stuff and jumped off the bus.

I scanned the parking lot and was relieved to see Junior's car. I headed straight for it and had the door closed before the bus was even done backfiring.

"What's up?" said Junior.

"Think I might have a problem," I said.

"All right," he said. "But did you guys win?"

"Yep, by twelve, but Bibo got hurt."

"Oof." He thought it over. "Well, one out of two ain't bad."

Later on, after I'd polished off some food and some homework, I gave Jammer a call. I needed to break the bad news about Bibo.

"Hey, man," I said.

The first thing he said, I kid you not: "Glad you called. I just heard back from Daniel. He's in! Now he can play with Braylon and the new guy, and Khalid can play with us. You, me, and Round Mound: There's no way we'll lose!"

At least Isaac had asked. This wasn't even a question. But I couldn't play for both teams. And what about my best friends?

Yeah, I thought, *I've definitely got a problem.*

CHAPTER 13

*I*t was Saturday morning. I wasn't sure which team I'd be on — and I wasn't the only one. New players were arriving at the practice court for the first time, and the atmosphere was electric.

The Bears were all charged up because Muni was there, and Muni was all charged up because the Bears were there. It didn't help that he'd arrived early and on his own. The first thing he said to me when I went over to shake his hand: "I got no backup!"

But then Fabrice arrived: big, tall Fabrice, who looked like a giant praying mantis. "Got my boy!" Muni called over. I gave him a thumbs-up and went back to helping piece the new teams together.

Unlike last week, the players had started showing up early. But they were all mismatched. In addition to all the new guys we'd invited, Bibo wasn't there and Benoit was.

He was the last of the "core guys," the one who hadn't been able to make it last time. "*That's* Benoit?" said Jammer. I was thinking the same thing. Overtime had invited him early, so we knew he was good. But he really didn't look like much. Not big, not small, not skinny, not fat — he just looked like a normal kid walking down the street.

"Well," I said, "guess we better find him a team."

I walked over to Kelvin and Isaac. "Hey, Amar'e," said Kelvin. "Muni's here! You're playing with us, right? Gotta stuff that fool!"

"Can't," I said. "All these new guys and stuff. I've got to ref and organize and everything else."

Isaac shook his head in that letdown way and said, "Well, who are we gonna play with? Joe?"

I looked over and saw Joe with Mike and Deuce, already talking strategy. "Nah," I said. "I need you guys to do me a favor. I've got someone new. Needs a team, supposed to be good."

"Hey, Benoit!" I called, and waved him over.

"*This* guy?" Kelvin said, and gave me the same look Jammer had.

"Trust me," I said, and hoped I was right.

The rest of the teams slowly got LEGO-blocked together. Two guys from the East Lake Lakers would latch onto a lone Eagle or Knight or Crimson Fury, whatever that is, and bam! You had a team. Two Crusaders from a Catholic school Jammer had played against joined forces with Walter.

Meanwhile, Stevie, who'd taken a tumble last time, was back in action today. He was hanging out with Khalid, Braylon, and Daniel. Jammer and I walked over to say hi.

"All right, Daniel's subbing in for me," said Khalid. "I'll play with you guys."

I looked around. "Wait, me?"

"Yeah, you, me, and Jammer."

"I thought I was reffing again," I said, looking at both of them.

"Numbers, man," said Khalid.

I looked around the court and did a quick

count. Seven groups of three — and then the three of us.

"Yeah," said Jammer. "We can all call our own fouls. It's a good group. That won't be a problem."

I looked over at Isaac and Kelvin. "I hope not," I said, but it was 9:15 already. Time to play.

We played first team to seven, and no win-by-two, either. The games went fast, and that was the plan. The idea was to have all the teams play one another at least once so winners rotated out just like everyone else.

It worked out pretty well because we all got to play some and scout out the other teams in between. The guy I was most interested in seeing was Benoit. He took to the court in the first game, along with Kelvin and Isaac. On the first possession, he hit a, well, I'm not even sure what to call it. It was kind of a spinning fade-away jump hook. Basically, it was an impossible shot, but he banked it off the backboard and right into the hoop.

"Well, that explains that," said Jammer.

Benoit kept taking circus shots and made enough of them to give him and his team a 7–5 win. I was hoping

Isaac and Kelvin would be happy with that, but they definitely didn't seem happy the next time they took the court — against me.

"Thought you were reffing," said Isaac.

"Numbers," I said with a shrug.

"Yeah, right," he said.

Yeah, definitely not happy. Kelvin didn't say anything, but he had a scowl on his face that let me know this probably wasn't the best game to drive down the lane.

They played hard, but first-to-seven happens fast. Khalid was at the top of his game, Jammer and I were hitting our shots, and we got a few good bounces. Just like that, it was 7–4 and we were off the court. All I could do was grab a drink of water and hope there wouldn't be any bad blood at Bears practice on Monday.

A game later, Muni's team took on Walter's. It was classic offense versus defense. It was also the longest 7–6 game I'd ever seen. Not a single car had shown up when it started, but half a dozen were waiting in the parking lot by the time Muni's long game-winner rattled in.

"Good practice," said Jammer as we headed toward the parking lot.

"Yeah," I said. "We finally have enough players."

"Just barely, but they're good ones."

"Definitely some good matchups," I said as a handful of paper was thrust in my face.

"Don't forget to take your flyers!"

It was Deuce. He was standing by the gate with a big grin on his face and a big stack of flyers under his arm. A few feet away, Mike had a stack of his own.

"Put 'em up around your school," he was saying, giving each player a handful as they headed home. "Give 'em to your folks!"

"Where'd you get all these copies?" I said.

Deuce kept smiling: "I'm not saying. But I hear that the copier in the main office is out of ink."

I shook my head: "They trust you way too much at that place."

He didn't say a word, just kept handing out flyers.

When I got home after practice, there was a letter waiting for me. It was on the table along with the bills and junk mail. My name and address were handwritten on the front. I opened it up.

Dear Amar'e,

I hope you are doing well. I would've called, but they won't let me! They took the telephone right out of my room. You met the nurse, but the doctor's even worse! They say they want me to relax and not worry about things until my blood pressure comes down. All this relaxation is driving me up a wall!

I hope everything is coming along with the Classic. I really appreciate you helping me out. That's the one thing that actually is helping me to relax: knowing that you and Jammer are out taking care of business.

I've got some good news, too. My leg is healing up fine, and the doc says I'll be out of here in time for tip-off. I can't wait to see some live hoops. Think you can get your hands on a nice MVP trophy? I'd love to hand one out at the end.

Thanks again for your help. It means a lot to this old man. If you want to write me back, you can send it care of the hospital. Who knows, that cranky old nurse might actually give it to me.

Your friend,

OT

Junior walked into the kitchen as I was folding the letter and putting it back into the envelope. "You getting bills now, too?" he said.

"It's a letter from Overtime," I said.

"Cool," he said, pouring himself some milk.

"Where do you get a really nice trophy, like an MVP trophy?"

Junior lowered the glass and wiped the milk mustache off his face with his forearm. "That's easy," he said. "You win it."

"Yeah, but what if you're the one handing it out?"

He thought about it. "That's tougher," he said. "Ask Dad." Then he drained the rest of the milk and walked out.

"Gee, thanks for your help!" I called after him.

CHAPTER 14

Bibo showed up at Bears practice on Monday in his big plastic walking boot. Everyone crowded around, looking at it and asking him questions.

Like I said before, Bibo definitely wasn't a big talker. He answered most of the questions by shrugging or pointing down at the boot.

"How does it feel?"

He shrugged.

"Is it heavy?"

He pointed.

"How easy is it to walk with?"

He took a few steps.

"Well, it's good to see you."

He smiled.

Then practice got started, and Bibo took a seat to watch. The first thing we did was partner up for a three-man defensive drill. Guess who partnered up with me right away. Yep, Isaac and Kelvin.

"What was that on Saturday?" said Isaac.

"Yeah, I thought you were just going to ref?"

"I was!" I said. "I mean, that's what I thought, but we had to fill out that last team."

"You could've played with us and let Benoit play with those other guys," said Isaac. It was totally true.

"It just worked out that way," I said. "What, you didn't like him? You won that first game pretty easy."

"Yeah, and we lost the second one — to you guys!" said Kelvin.

"And he's a chucker, man," said Isaac. "He just throws it up from anywhere."

We were still running the drill as we were saying all this, and starting to huff and puff as we talked. "Yeah, but he makes a lot of those shots."

"Yeah, and he misses the rest," said Isaac. "Meanwhile,

K-man here is the biggest guy on the court, and Benoit's not even trying to work it down low to him."

I had to admit that was a good point. The drill was almost over.

"So you'll play with us at the Classic, right?" said Kelvin.

"Yeah, we need an all-Bears team out there," said Isaac. I thought of Joe, but Mike and D really seemed to like playing with him.

"Maybe," I said. It was time to level with them. "Jammer and Khalid want me to play with them, too. That was the plan going in."

Isaac looked at Kelvin and then back at me.

"But those guys have tons of tourney experience," he said. "This is our first one. We need to represent — and you invited us."

Those were good points, too.

"I'll think about it," I said, and I meant it. Maybe Benoit could play with Jammer and Khalid. It would definitely be a tough team to defend. The whistle blew. The drill was over, but I felt like I was still playing defense.

On Tuesday night, Carl drove Jammer and me out to check out the court. We had to figure out where we were going to sell tickets, where the tables would go and the teams would stretch out, and all that stuff.

The guy who ran the place was waiting there for us when we arrived. His name was Mr. Tompkins. He probably had a first name, too, but I never found out what it was. He was one of those old dudes who was basically just a "Mister." We talked to him for a while about the sound system, then Jammer and I walked around the court and tried to get a handle on things.

"There's supposed to be an MVP trophy, too," I said.

"Oh, man, I forgot about that," said Jammer. "Where are we going to get one now? We've got no budget."

"I'll ask my dad about it. He'll know."

"Hope so," said Jammer. "Hey, let's put the scorer's table here, with the microphone right on it."

"Yeah," I said, "that'll work."

We talked about a lot of little things, but I was having trouble bringing up that one last big thing: who I'd play with. I guess I didn't want to rock the boat. I was the one who'd shot my mouth off and said we'd put the Classic together, but Jammer had jumped right in to help out. He was a good friend, and I didn't want to let him down.

It was getting late. Mr. Tompkins turned on the big lights so we could see how things would look on Saturday night. "Let's play some one-on-one," said Jammer. "Just to test it out."

"Good idea," I said as Jammer produced a scuffed-up basketball from his backpack.

He tossed the backpack aside and got down into a low dribble. I pulled my goggles out from the case in my pocket, tugged on my shorts, and got down into a defensive stance. The only sounds were the ball bouncing, the hum of the lights, and the thick bass coming from the open window of Carl's car. He was sitting in the driver's seat with his head turned to watch us play. Out of the corner of my eye, I saw Mr. Tompkins take a front-row seat on the bleachers.

I tuned them out and focused on Jammer. We had an audience now, and I didn't want to get posterized. For a few beats, his dribble matched the beat of the music. If he kept it up, I could reach out and steal the ball with no problem. But he realized it a drumbeat after I did and switched it up.

"Nice try," he said. "You almost —" He took off in the middle of his sentence, trying to catch me napping. I didn't fall for it. I knew all his tricks! As soon as he realized he wasn't going to turn the corner on me, he pulled it back. Then he started trying to back me in.

Jammer was a year older than me, but not that much bigger. He tried to back me in but I held my ground, and he got tired of that. He swung the ball around to face the basket, keeping his dribble alive. He was closer to the rim now, and I took a few swipes at the ball to keep him from getting too comfortable.

He tried a head fake, then a shoulder fake, looking for any little opening. I stayed low and didn't give him one. He pulled the ball back a little and seemed to be considering his next move. He had this look on his face like, *Huh, what now?*

And of course, that's when he rose up and fired off a short fadeaway. I rose up out of my crouch and waved at it, but the ball just cleared my fingertips. I turned

around to box him out, but there was no rebound. The ball hit the backboard and dropped through.

"Nice," I said. "I never saw a face fake before."

"I still got a few tricks up my sleeve," he said.

"You're not wearing sleeves," I said, nodding at his tank top.

"That's what makes it so surprising," he said.

We just kept on like that for a while. He scored a few, and I scored a few. We weren't really keeping score. Sometimes Mr. Tompkins would say, "All right, now," when one of us did something good, or he'd make a little clucking sound when one of us got burned or threw up a brick. We could just hear it over the music, and after a while, we started playing for those "All right, nows" — or at least to avoid those clucks.

We got a good rhythm going and a little bit of a sweat, and then I got around the corner on Jammer. It was just a quick first step and off to the races, but we'd been giving each other so many jab steps and fakes that he didn't believe I was going until I was already gone. I had a clear path to the hoop. Dunking was still pretty new to me, and I needed some room for takeoff. I wasn't sure I had enough, but with a crowd of two and under the lights, I figured why not.

One more dribble and I went up strong — and powered it down!

"*All right, now!*" said Mr. Tompkins.

"Got ya there, cuz!" called Carl.

Jammer just shook his head. "All right," he said, "you asked for it. I've got a new move I've been saving for a special occasion. Prepare to get thrown down on!"

"Sure," I said. I thought he was bluffing, but nope. He blew by me a few plays later with a slithery, snake of a move I'd never seen before. The rim rattled as he threw down a one-hander. They didn't call him Jammer for nothing!

"Save something for the Classic," I said.

"Yeah, you too," he said. "We are going to monsterize out there."

"Oh yeah," I said. Just like that I realized I had to let him know what was up. It was easier than I thought. I don't know why. I guess maybe it's because a good one-on-one game is almost like a conversation, anyway.

"I know I played with you guys on Saturday," I said. "But I don't know about the tourney."

"What d'you mean?" said Jammer. He narrowed his eyes and gave me a look, but he didn't pick up his dribble. "You, me, and Khalid, man: It's the dream team."

"Yeah, I know, but I'm getting some pressure from my boys."

"From your Bears, you mean."

"Yeah, I'm having some Bear trouble," I admitted. "But they've got a point."

"What, 'cause Bibo went down?"

"Yeah, that's part of it, but our biggest rivals are playing, too, the guys from Central."

"Yeah, those guys are good," admitted Jammer. "Muni can shoot it."

"Yeah, and if the Bears lose to them? And it's Benoit instead of me out there? It won't be pretty. And Benoit was firing it up like crazy, anyway."

Jammer was still dribbling nice and slow. He tried a few moves, just to see if I'd bite, but mostly we were just talking now. "Yeah, I saw that," he said. "I think he was just making up for lost time, 'cause he missed the first practice. He's a good player."

"Yeah, I know it, but the guys want to play with someone they know."

"Well, so do I," said Jammer. For the first time, I thought I heard a little edge in his voice.

"Hey, I'd love to play with you and Khalid. I just . . . it's a tough call."

Jammer crossed the ball over and gave it a few loud, hard dribbles. He wasn't happy about this. Not at all.

"If I could," I said, "I'd play with both teams."

"But you can't," he said, and drove hard to the hoop.

CHAPTER 15

"I can't believe it's Wednesday already!" I said.

"Yeah, that seems to happen every week," said Deuce.

Mike was too busy chewing his lunch to chime in. We were sitting around our usual table in the cafeteria and strategizing. Ever since they made those flyers, Mike and Deuce sort of considered themselves the publicity committee. And with only three days to go before the tournament, I definitely needed the help.

"What about the newspaper?" said Deuce.

"Already sent something in to their calendar section," I said.

"You hear back?" said Mike in between bites.

"Not yet."

"What about the radio station?" said Deuce.

"What — the little local one?" I said.

"Yeah, they do a calendar thing, too, like 'Things to Do This Weekend,' or something like that. Think they even have a sports program."

"Oh yeah," I said. "Dad has that on in the truck sometimes. Good idea."

"Want me to check with them, see if they'll mention the Classic?" said Deuce.

"Yeah, that would be great," I said. "I'm completely swamped with all the other stuff."

"As long as you're ready to play on Saturday," said Mike. He'd just finished his lunch in no time flat and was eyeing what was left on Deuce's tray.

"I'm definitely ready," I said. "After all this work, I can't wait to get out there and actually play. I just don't know who I'm playing with. . . ."

As soon as I said it, the table got quiet. And not a good kind of quiet, either. Deuce looked at Mike, Mike looked at Deuce, and then they both looked at me.

"Wait a second," said Deuce. "I thought you were playing with us."

I couldn't believe it! This was the last thing I needed.

"Yeah," said Mike. "I thought that was the deal when you invited us."

They both gave me these looks of total betrayal. I felt really bad and then . . . the corner of Mike's mouth started to twitch. Then Deuce's cheeks filled with air.

And they both burst out laughing!

"Oh, man!" said Mike. "You should've seen your face!"

"Talk about a Classic," said Deuce. "That was classic!"

"That was pretty good," I admitted. I imitated their super-serious faces and we all cracked up again.

Once things settled down, Deuce said: "But seriously, I thought you were playing with Jammer and Round Mound?"

"Yeah, that's what I thought, too. But now Bibo's out and Isaac and Kelvin are putting the pressure on. They want an all-Bears team to win it all — or at least take out the guys from Central."

"Well," said Mike. "You are a Bear."

I shot him a look.

"Whoa," he said. "I'm not saying you should play with them. I'm just saying: You are on the team."

"Sorry, Mike," I said. "I didn't mean that. I just don't know what to do about it. It seems like I should play for both teams, but I can't."

"Well, you don't have to worry about us," said Deuce. "I mean, it would be awesome if the three of us could play. It's like the original crew. But we know you've got responsibilities, and Joe's been cool."

"Thanks, guys," I said.

"No problem," said Deuce. "Just my opinion, but as much work as you've put in, I think you should be able to play with whoever you want to."

"Yeah, no problem," said Mike, and then he kind of paused. I could tell he had something else to say. I thought it might be some more good advice or something, so I leaned in close.

"Gonna eat that cookie?"

We got another good laugh out of that, but as I handed it over, I realized something. I already had all the advice I needed.

I didn't even make it to practice on Thursday before Isaac and Kelvin asked me who I was planning to play with. They came over as I was changing in the locker room.

"Made up your mind yet?" said Isaac.

"Yep," I said, and I told them. It was a pretty simple case to make.

I finished tying my sneakers and then looked up to see their reaction. They were nodding.

"So we're good?" I said.

"Yeah," said Kelvin. "We're good."

As soon as I got home, I heard from Jammer. I told him the same thing.

"Yeah," he said, thinking it over. "That works for me."

It felt good to be out of the doghouse, especially since there was still so much to do. We had the courts and the teams, and it felt like there was at least a chance that there'd be a crowd there to see it all. But there were still lots of little details to iron out. Like did we need actual tickets or a hand stamp or could we just go with the honor system?

Jammer and I talked it all over, but I still felt like there was something I was forgetting. I was about to find out. Friday flew by, and just like that, it was tourney time!

Dad knocked off work early so we could lug some stuff to the court.

"What's this for?" he said as he slid an old folding table across the tailgate and toward where I was kneeling in the back of the truck.

"This is the scorer's table," I said. "And we'll have the microphone and the trophies on it."

And then it hit me: "Oh no! I forgot the trophy!"

"What trophy?" said Dad.

"The MVP trophy! Overtime asked me about it in his letter. He said he was looking forward to handing it out. I've been so busy all week, I just forgot!"

It was a disaster. There was a clean blue tarp next to me in the truck bed. The idea was to use it to make the table look more official, but right then I just wanted to hide underneath it. How could I make such a huge mistake? There was no time to get a trophy now.

"This is terrible," I said. "OT is going to be really bummed."

Dad shook his head. "It sounds pretty bad," he admitted. "But there's nothing for it now. Better just climb down out of there and help me load this one last thing."

"Okay," I said, but I barely heard him. I sleepwalked to the edge of the tailgate and hopped down into the driveway. Then I turned and followed Dad into the garage. The whole time I was trying to figure out how this happened. I remembered telling Jammer I'd ask my dad about it. But then there was that one-on-one game and all that drama. And then all the publicity to take care of . . .

Dad handed me a heavy hunk of wood and metal, but I barely looked at it. "Where's this go?" I mumbled.

"Might as well put it on top of that table," he said. "I think that's where you said the trophies go."

I looked up. "What are you talking about?" He had a big, goofy grin on his face. Then I looked at the thing in my hand. It was a shiny brass basketball-player statue on top of a heavy wooden base. Expertly carved into the front of the wood were three big letters: *MVP*. It was the nicest trophy I'd ever seen!

"Where?" I said. "How?" I could barely get the words out I was so surprised.

"You asked Junior where to get an MVP trophy, remember?" said Dad. "And he asked me. Wasn't too hard to figure out."

"And you just . . . made one?"

"Yeah, your old man knows a thing or two, you know. That's cherry wood there, and that decoration on top? Believe it or not, that came from one of Junior's old trophies. It fell off and I had it in a drawer in the garage."

I just stood there for a few seconds, looking at his workshop masterpiece and trying to pick my jaw up off the driveway. "You made me a trophy. . . ."

"No," said Dad firmly. "I made the MVP of the Classic a trophy. We'll see who that is in a few hours. Now hurry up and get it in the truck or we're going to be late."

"Dad," I said. "Thanks doesn't even cover it."

"I know," he said, "but it'll do."

I was afraid the trophy would get scuffed up in the back of the truck, so I brought it with me as I climbed into the passenger seat. The preparations were officially done. Without another word, we buckled up and headed for the court.

CHAPTER 16

Carl and Jammer were already there when we arrived, and we immediately started unloading the truck and setting everything up. Mr. Tompkins was walking around making sure everything was working.

"Sweet trophy!" said Jammer as I handed it to him. "We'll put it right in the center here so everyone knows what they're playing for. And so they'll be jealous when I win it!"

"You wish," I said. "But I might let you hold it after I win it!"

Meanwhile, Carl was setting up the little ticket table by the entrance, and Dad and Mr. Tompkins were discussing the finer points of setting up electrical wiring outside. And just as I was taking a look around at the usual cast, I saw an unusual cast heading right for us. A familiar figure walked through the main gate, with the help of a crutch and a fat white cast on his leg.

"Overtime!" I called, and Jammer and I ran over to see him.

"Hey, boys!" he said. "It's great to see you. I'm pretty sure I recognize this court, too. 'Course my view is a little different this time, not rolling around in pain and all."

"Yeah," said Jammer. "Hope that's okay. It was the best one we could get."

"Oh, no, it's fine," said Overtime. "It's a good court — and it owes me one!"

"Yeah, how are you feeling?" I said.

"I feel a lot better now that I'm out of that hospital!" he said. "Nice to see the sun again."

I looked over. The sun was reddish orange and sinking toward the horizon. When I turned back around, I saw three more guys walking through the gate. I recognized them all. Two were regular volunteers at OT's tournaments, and the third was one of his regular refs. All three were carrying boxes.

That was OT for you: out of the hospital for two hours and already working his magic. "Let's get to it," he said to the men. "We've got an hour to make this place presentable!"

And just like that, they started putting up banners and decorations, pulling out stacks of forms, raffle tickets, smaller trophies for the teams, and everything else that made up a successful tournament. I let out a long, slow breath. For the first time in weeks, I felt myself relax. Really relax. The tournament was in good hands. Now all I had to worry about was playing hoops. And that I knew I could handle.

The late day shadows grew longer as we put the final touches on the court. By the time people started to show up, everything was in place. Pretty soon it went from a few early birds arriving to a steady stream of players, families, and basketball fans. Some of them were holding the flyers that Mike and Deuce had made. Others had read about it in the newspaper or heard the news on the radio.

"This is terrific," said Overtime, watching the long line of people handing over money at the ticket table and then filing into the stands, filling up row after row. "I hate to say it, but I had a few nightmares when I got here and it was just the three of us."

Jammer and I laughed.

"I had the same one!" I admitted.

"In mine, it was just the two of you," said Jammer. "Because I was running late!"

We all took one last look at the stands, nearly full now. I saw Dad up there with Manny and a few other guys from his crew. And heading down the row to join them were Junior and a few of his friends. They were all doing their part to help fill the seats. I gave them a quick wave.

Then OT headed over to the scorer's table, and Jammer and I headed out to the court with the rest of the players. It was time to warm up for the first round of action. All the games would be single elimination: Winners advance, losers sit. One and done.

It was finally time to join my team.

* * *

"You ready, guys?" I said to my teammates as we took the court for our first game.

"Ready," said Deuce.

"As I'll ever be," said Mike.

So yeah, that was my team. The choice between Jammer and Khalid and the Bears was a tough one. But once I thought of it, the choice to play with my best friends was easy. They were the ones who'd been with me all along, the ones who got me ready for my first tournament and every one since then. They were just here to play for fun, and you know what? After all the work that went into putting things together, so was I. To me, this one was about helping Overtime make the Classic happen, and I'd done everything I could. Now I was going to play some ball with my best friends and see how far we could go.

We lined up for the tip. Across from us were Walter and those two fierce defenders. It was our first-round matchup and we'd drawn Team Lock-Down. I knelt down and sort of bounced on my knees a few times, getting ready for the jump.

A few feet away, Walter did the same thing. The last

rays of the Florida sun lit the court, and a single drop of sweat slowly made its way down my forehead. Suddenly, the ref tossed the ball high into the air.

Walter and I flew up to get it like a pair of falcons. My wingspan was a little longer, and I tipped the ball back to Deuce. The other team slapped on their airtight man-to-man defense as we headed up court.

After a few scoreless possessions for both teams, we knew we were in for a battle. At a lot of tourneys, you'd play to a specific score: first team to twenty-one or whatever. At the Classic, we were playing ten-minute games in the first round. It was a good thing, too. At this rate, it would take us all night to reach twenty-one.

Deuce whipped the ball to me as we headed back up the court, but Walter got a hand on it and tipped it out of bounds. The ball rolled under the bleachers. We huddled up quickly while a kid climbed under there to get it.

"Man, my guy is strong," said Mike. "I swear he must've spent every minute since the last practice doing push-ups or something."

"And my guy is fast," said Deuce.

I nodded. Walter was some of both.

"And they're super-disciplined: never out of position," Deuce added.

The kid emerged from under the bleachers with the ball and the crowd cheered. The ref took the ball and headed toward the sideline. Our time was almost up.

"Maybe we should be, then," I said.

"We should be what?" said Mike.

"Out of position," I said.

"Seriously?" said Deuce.

"Yeah, let's just mix it up. Have some fun, like we do when we're messing around at the old court in the park."

"It's worth a shot," said Deuce.

When we inbounded the ball, we took to the court with a whole new attitude. You've probably heard of a pick-and-roll. So had the other team. They played them perfectly and never seemed to get out of position. But have you heard of a pick-and-pick-and-roll? Nope, and Walter and his teammates hadn't, either!

It was basically a crazy play that Mike, Deuce, and I had drawn up in the dirt during a long pickup game down at our local court. It worked then, and it worked again. For the first time, a team that was always in the right position had no right position to be in. They were all jumbled up near the free throw line as I slipped to the hoop with my hand up. Deuce got me the ball and — one finger roll later — we were on the board.

Thirty seconds later, we introduced them to the drive-and-dish-and-dish-and-drive! As expected, they defended the first part perfectly. Mike drove down the lane like a bull running down hill. His defender had no trouble staying in front of him, and Mike tossed the ball out to me on the perimeter.

And of course Walter was on me like a glove. He'd been expecting Mike to pass it out. What he wasn't expecting was that Deuce would be cutting to the hoop at the same moment. He flew down the lane, a half step ahead of his defender. Mike was already in position to pin his own defender behind him under the hoop. Now I did my part.

Instead of taking the shot, I fired the ball back into the lane. Deuce hauled it in and lofted up a floater for our second bucket. After that, we had them off-balance. We wound up winning pretty easily, 17–11.

We shook hands and headed to the bleachers to watch the rest of the first-round action. First up, Jammer, Khalid, and their new teammate, Benoit. Since he was the other "core guy" OT had invited, he was an obvious pick to take my place. And this time it was obvious to everyone why.

He wasn't hoisting up circus shots the way he had at the first practice. He was playing smart, but he could still hit from just about anywhere on the court. Add in Jammer's athleticism and Khalid's quickness, and they had no trouble beating Hector, Lex, and Van and advancing. Afterward, Jammer came and sat by me on the bench.

"Nice game," I said.

"Yeah, you too," he said. "Those were some crazy plays you guys made out there."

"Had to," I said. "The non-crazy ones weren't working!"

The whistle blew for the next teams to take the court. I watched this one carefully, too. Isaac and Kelvin had what they wanted: an all-Bears team. Joe lined up in front of them for the tip.

They were playing Daniel, Stevie, and Braylon. Those guys were all tournament veterans, so it was a tough matchup. "Let's go, Bears!" I shouted.

The game was close the whole way, but Kelvin was just too big. Isaac kept dumping the ball into him down low and he pretty much worked Stevie over. Daniel could do a lot of things for his team, but he couldn't make them grow any bigger. In the end, it was Bears by two.

Three of the four second-round teams were set. Just a few minutes into the next game, it was clear who'd get the last slot. Muni was on his game. He seemed almost bored out there as he drained one shot after another from the outside. He kept it up and by the end it was one dagger after another.

"Man," said Jammer, shaking his head as Muni put the other team away with icy precision.

"Man," I echoed.

We were both thinking the same thing. Someone's going to have to face that guy in the next round.

CHAPTER 17

*T*he team that had to try to cool down Muni in Round 2 was . . . the Bears! I had all kinds of bad thoughts as the six players took the court. Well, maybe not all kinds. Basically, I had one bad thought: They might lose and then blame me for not being on the team.

Either way, I settled in to watch the fireworks. The first thing I noticed was that Muni didn't look bored anymore. He looked determined. This was the grudge match both teams had been waiting for: Bears versus Cougars. I turned to say something to Jammer about it, but he was gone. I knew the score there, too.

If the Bears were playing Muni's squad, that meant my team was taking on Jammer's. The two winners would play in the championship game. Jammer and Khalid were my friends, but now they were my opponents, too. I caught a glimpse of them farther down the bench, leaning in and whispering something to Benoit. They were probably telling him every last thing about my game.

As usual, Deuce read my mind. "So, Jammer's crew, huh?" he said.

I nodded.

"Tough matchup," said Mike.

"No doubt," I said.

The game got started out on the court. The lights were on now, and Overtime was calling the action from over at the scorer's table. Everything felt more charged and electric now that we were in the second round. The crowd felt it, too, cheering the scores and booing the fouls, oohing and aahing at the most exciting plays. And there were a lot of those.

Muni was still doing his thing, just not quite as often. The Bears knew his tricks better than anyone here, and Joe was a tough defender. Meanwhile, Kelvin and Fabrice were battling down low. K-man was bigger, but Fabrice was taller. Every rebound was war.

With Bibo out, I was wondering where the Bears would get most of their points. Isaac answered that with his first warp-speed drive down the lane. I leaned in closer. I'd never seen him operate like this. I was used to him setting up Bibo or me, or maybe dumping it to Kelvin. Now he was looking to score and using his speed to do it.

The game stayed close. With a few minutes left, I knew I should be talking strategy with Mike and Deuce, but I couldn't peel my eyes away. The Bears were my friends, too — and my teammates at school. And the Cougars were my rivals.

It all came down to defense. The Bears were up by one, but Muni had the ball with a handful of seconds left. Joe was playing him tight, like he had all game. Muni jabbed his left foot forward, looking to create some space. Then he stepped back for the shot.

Joe didn't bite. He'd seen that move before in the game we'd played against the Cougars. He stayed tight and forced Muni to adjust his shot. And that's how it goes, you know? Sometimes games end with a swish and sometimes they end with a clang. The ball hit the front rim and bounced away. Bears win!

I was still cheering when the ref came over to Mike, Deuce, and me. "Five minutes till the tip," he said.

I looked over at Jammer's crew, still talking strategy. Then I looked at Mike and D. We had to make up for lost time. We huddled up and I started telling them everything I knew about Jammer and Khalid. Toward the end, I concentrated on just telling Deuce about Khalid's best moves and tricks. I'd guard Jammer myself. As for Mike, I looked over at Benoit and told him what he already knew: "You're bigger than that guy. If he wants to take those circus shots outside, I say we let him and you just vacuum up the rebounds."

"You sure?" said Mike.

I considered our options. That whole team could score, and there was no way Mike could hang with Benoit on the outside.

"I think it's our best shot," I said.

We all looked at one another.

"Our best shot," said Deuce.

Mike and I repeated it. Then we put our hands in the center of the huddle: "One, two, three . . . Go, team!" And we took the court.

Before I get to the score and all of that, let me just say one thing: We battled! The guys on Jammer's team were a year or two older than we were, and they were tourney vets, "core guys," the best of the best.

What were we? Best friends and fearless! And, all right, I was a "core guy," too. I hung tough with Jammer all game. It was a little weird because I'd learned so much of my game from him. But I'd learned it well, and I could match his size and hops.

The score was tied early, and we were playing well. Jammer had the ball at the top of the key, and I was in front of him with good position. He threw a couple of little fakes my way, but I stayed squared up in front of him and he gave the ball up.

I didn't exactly make him do it. He just realized something: Why go toe-to-toe with me when there are easier opportunities all around? He passed the ball to

Benoit a few steps outside the lane. If he was out a little farther, Mike would've let him take the shot, like we'd talked about. But Benoit was too close — and too good — to leave alone now. Mike jumped out to guard him.

I saw a flash of movement out of the corner of my eye. "Watch out, Deuce!" I called, but it was too late. Khalid had already turned the corner. And by stepping out, Mike had opened up the lane. Khalid scored the way a cobra strikes: so fast you almost wonder if it really happened.

It really happened. That was the moment I knew how this was going to play out. I could hang with Jammer — I even scored one more bucket than him. But my teammates just didn't have the experience to match these vets yet.

We kept it close enough. Toward the end, I started feeding Mike and Deuce, looking to get them some more buckets before the end. And then the time was up — and our run was over.

"Good game, man," I said after the air horn went off, reaching out to shake Jammer's hand.

He looked down at my hand and shook his head: *No.* That kind of surprised me. I thought we were cool. And then he hugged me. It was an awkward, guy hug, but still. It surprised me even more.

"You're a warrior, man," he said. Then he walked over to shake hands with Mike and D, and I did the same with Khalid and Benoit.

Now that the final game was set, everyone was buzzing about the showdown between the tourney vets and the Bears. A food cart had shown up right as the tournament was starting. We'd steered clear of it while we still had games to play, but now we were ready to chow down.

I walked up into the bleachers to get some money. I got some pats on the back and "Good games" on the way up.

"Hey, Dad," I said when I reached his row. "Can I borrow a few bucks?"

"You can have 'em," he said. "I'm proud of you, son."

"I lost," I said.

He shook his head. "That's not what I'm talking about."

"Good game, anyway," said Junior, and we bumped fists.

"Nice goggles," said Manny, and I laughed, since they were just like the ones he wore to work. Then I handed my goggles to Dad for safekeeping and headed back down to Mike and D.

Deuce got two hot dogs, and Mike got three (of course). I wasn't so down with the mystery meat, but I got a jumbo-size hot pretzel. Then we found seats in the front row after the other players shoved over and made some room.

As the game started, I couldn't help thinking that I could be on either one of those teams. I could be playing for the Classic title right now. But then I looked to one side and saw Mike chowing down and cheering at the same time. I looked to the other and saw Deuce, so into the game he didn't realize he had a big glob of ketchup on his shorts. I looked past them and saw the other players, still here after they'd been eliminated, still cheering. I saw all that and I knew I'd made the right decision.

And the game? It was a good one, but I don't think anyone was too surprised when Jammer's team pulled away toward the end. Both teams left the court smiling, anyway. The veterans had won it all, but the Bears had made it to the end — and beaten Muni along the way.

The long night was almost over. All that was left was presenting the MVP trophy at center court. I headed out to get a better view. I had plenty of time. Overtime was still hobbling around the table, so I angled over that way.

"Need any help, OT?" I said.

"All I can get," he said. "But for starters, could you grab the trophy?"

"Sure," I said. I plucked Dad's MVP trophy off the scorer's table, and we headed out onto the court, nice and slow.

I looked down at the beautiful wood and brass trophy as I went. I was going to be sad to hand it over.

CHAPTER 18

Overtime's deep voice reverberated through the microphone: "And the MVP award for the twentieth annual edition of the Classic goes to . . ."

The crowd had made its way down from the bleachers and onto the court all around us. Now they leaned in for the announcement — even though they could probably hear it in the next town over.

"James Jamison, or as you probably know him — Jammer!"

The crowd cheered. It was no surprise. He'd been the best player on the best team. He deserved it. I was a little disappointed not to win, but mostly I was happy for Jammer.

I held out the trophy — but I wasn't the only one doing that. One of the volunteers who'd showed up with Overtime was holding out another trophy. Jammer walked over and took that one.

Overtime must've seen the look of total confusion on my face, because he sort of interrupted himself. "Now, just a second, just a second," he said. "I'm going to ask Jammer to say a few words in a moment, but first I want to clear something up. Some of you are probably wondering why we've got one MVP and two trophies out here today."

I knew I was. I looked at OT and nodded like a bobblehead.

"Well, that's because we don't have one MVP," he said. "We have two!"

There were a few whoops from the crowd and then Overtime went on. "There's a young man here today. Now, his team didn't win it all, but he played hard and he played well. But more important than all of that, I can honestly say, if it wasn't for him, this tournament never would have happened."

There was a buzzing in my ears. I could see a few dozen eyes turn toward me.

"Amar'e," said Overtime, nodding toward the trophy in my hands. "You can keep that. You earned it."

The crowd cheered. I was so surprised that I just stood there with my mouth open. I was lucky I didn't catch any flies!

"Now, Jammer, you want to say a few words?"

Jammer took the mic. "Uh, yes, sir. I'd just like to say" — he looked around at the crowd and then pointed back toward Overtime — "I agree with what he said!"

The crowd laughed. He handed the mic back to Overtime, and took his trophy back out from under his arm. Then he turned to me and said, "You ready, STAT? On the count of three: one . . . two . . ."

I knew exactly what he meant. I closed my mouth into a big smile and waited for "three." When he said it, we both raised our trophies high over our heads. The crowd went bonkers, and you know what? I kind of did, too.

It wasn't just the trophy; it was what it represented. It was everything that went into it, everything and

everyone. They were all around me now, my friends and my family.

With a crutch in one hand and the mic in the other, it took OT a while to make it over to me. "You have anything you want to say, Amar'e?"

He handed me the microphone. I put the trophy under my arm and took it. "Yes, there's something I've been meaning to ask all day."

The crowd got silent, waiting to hear what burning question I had on my mind.

"Can I sign your cast?"

There was laughter all around us. Overtime looked down at the shiny white cast on his leg. There wasn't a single signature on it. Then he looked up to see the whole crowd inching toward him. I saw his Adam's apple move: *Gulp!* He knew that once the signing started, we'd be here for a while.

That was fine with me. It would give me a chance to thank everyone I needed to: my family, my friends, my rivals — and you, too. Thanks for reading my books!

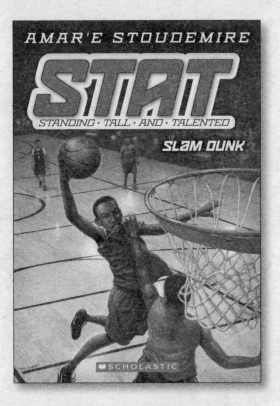

BRING YOUR A GAME OR GET SCHOOLED!

CLASS IS IN SESSION!

CHECK OUT STAT #4: SCHOOLED.